THE DREAM OF THE
RED CHAMBER

Cao Xueqin

The Dream of the
Red Chamber

Translated by David Hawkes

PENGUIN BOOKS

PENGUIN BOOKS

Published by the Penguin Group
Penguin Books USA Inc., 375 Hudson Street,
New York, New York 10014, U.S.A.
Penguin Books Ltd, 27 Wrights Lane, London W8 5 TZ, England
Penguin Books Australia Ltd, Ringwood, Victoria, Australia
Penguin Books Canada Ltd, 10 Alcorn Avenue,
Toronto, Ontario, Canada, M4V 3B2
Penguin Books (N.Z.) Ltd, 182–190 Wairau Road,
Auckland 10, New Zealand

Penguin Books Ltd, Registered Offices:
Harmondsworth, Middlesex, England

Published in Penguin Books 1995

This selection is from Cao Xueqin's *The Story of the Stone, Volume 1, The Golden Days*, translated by David Hawkes, published by Penguin Books.

ISBN 0 14 60.0176 1

Printed in the United States of America

THE DREAM OF THE RED CHAMBER

Zhen Shi-yin makes the Stone's acquaintance in a dream

GENTLE READER,

What, you may ask, was the origin of this book?

Though the answer to this question may at first seem to border on the absurd, reflection will show that there is a good deal more in it than meets the eye.

Long ago, when the goddess Nü-wa was repairing the sky, she melted down a great quantity of rock and, on the Incredible Crags of the Great Fable Mountains, moulded the amalgam into thirty-six thousand, five hundred and one large building blocks, each measuring seventy-two feet by a hundred and forty-four feet square. She used thirty-six thousand five hundred of these blocks in the course of her building operations, leaving a single odd block unused, which lay, all on its own, at the foot of Greensickness Peak in the afore-mentioned mountains.

Now this block of stone, having undergone the melting and moulding of a goddess, possessed magic powers. It could move about at will and could grow or shrink to any size it wanted. Observing that all the other blocks had been used for celestial repairs and that it was the only one to have been rejected as unworthy, it became filled with shame and resentment and passed its days in sorrow and lamentation.

One day, in the midst of its lamentings, it saw a monk and a Taoist approaching from a great distance, each of them remarkable for certain eccentricities of manner and appearance. When they arrived at the foot of Greensickness Peak, they sat down on the ground and began to talk. The monk, catching sight of a lustrous, translucent stone—it was in fact the rejected building block which had now shrunk itself to the size of a fan-pendant and looked very attractive in its new shape—took it up on the palm of his hand and addressed it with a smile:

'Ha, I see you have magical properties! But nothing to recommend you. I shall have to cut a few words on you so that anyone seeing you will know at once that you are something special. After that I shall take you to a certain

brilliant
successful
poetical
cultivated
aristocratic
elegant
delectable
luxurious
opulent
locality on a little trip.'

The stone was delighted.

'What words will you cut? Where is this place you will take me to? I beg to be enlightened.'

'Do not ask,' replied the monk with a laugh. 'You will know soon enough when the time comes.'

And with that he slipped the stone into his sleeve and set off at a great pace with the Taoist. But where they both went to I have no idea.

Countless aeons went by and a certain Taoist called Vanitas in quest of the secret of immortality chanced to be passing below that same Greensickness Peak in the Incredible Crags of the Great Fable Mountains when he caught sight of a large stone standing there, on which the characters of a long inscription were clearly discernible.

Vanitas read the inscription through from beginning to end and learned that this was a once lifeless stone block which had been found unworthy to repair the sky, but which had magically transformed its shape and been taken down by the Buddhist mahāsattva Impervioso and the Taoist illuminate Mysterioso into the world of mortals, where it had lived out the life of a man before finally attaining nirvana and returning to the other shore. The inscription named the country where it had been born, and went into considerable detail about its domestic life, youthful amours, and even the verses, mottoes and riddles it had written. All it lacked was the authentication of a dynasty and date. On the back of the stone was inscribed the following quatrain:

> Found unfit to repair the azure sky
> Long years a foolish mortal man was I.
> My life in both worlds on this stone is writ:
> Pray who will copy out and publish it?

From his reading of the inscription Vanitas realized that this was a stone of some consequence. Accordingly he addressed himself to it in the following manner:

'Brother Stone, according to what you yourself seem to imply in these verses, this story of yours contains matter of sufficient interest to merit publication and has been carved here with that end in view. But as far as I can see (a) it has no discoverable dynastic period, and (b) it contains no examples of moral grandeur among its characters—no statesmanship, no social message of any kind. All I can find in it, in fact, are a number of females, conspicuous, if at all, only for their passion or folly or for some trifling talent or insignificant virtue. Even if I were to copy all this out, I cannot see that it would make a very remarkable book.'

'Come, your reverence,' said the stone (for Vanitas had been correct in assuming that it could speak) 'must you be so obtuse? All the romances ever written have an artificial period setting—Han or Tang for the most part. In refusing to make use of that stale old convention and telling my *Story of the Stone* exactly as it occurred, it seems to me that, far from *depriving* it of anything, I have given it a freshness these other books do not have.

'Your so-called "historical romances", consisting, as they do, of scandalous anecdotes about statesmen and emperors of bygone days and scabrous attacks on the reputations of long-dead gentlewomen, contain more wickedness and immorality than I care to mention. Still worse is the "erotic novel", by whose filthy obscenities our young folk are all too easily corrupted. And the "boudoir romances", those dreary stereotypes with their volume after volume all pitched on the same note and their different characters indistinguishable except by name (all those ideally beautiful young ladies and ideally eligible young bachelors)—even they seem unable to avoid descending sooner or later into indecency.

'The trouble with this last kind of romance is that it only gets written in the first place because the author requires a framework in which to show off his love-poems. He goes about constructing this framework quite mechanically, beginning with the names of his pair of young lovers and invariably adding a third character, a servant or the like, to make mischief between them, like the *chou* in a comedy.

6

'What makes these romances even more detestable is the stilted, bombastic language—inanities dressed in pompous rhetoric, remote alike from nature and common sense and teeming with the grossest absurdities.

'Surely my "number of females", whom I spent half a lifetime studying with my own eyes and ears, are preferable to this kind of stuff? I do not claim that they are better people than the ones who appear in books written before my time; I am only saying that the contemplation of their actions and motives may prove a more effective antidote to boredom and melancholy. And even the inelegant verses with which my story is interlarded could serve to entertain and amuse on those convivial occasions when rhymes and riddles are in demand.

'All that my story narrates, the meetings and partings, the joys and sorrows, the ups and downs of fortune, are recorded exactly as they happened. I have not dared to add the tiniest bit of touching-up, for fear of losing the true picture.

'My only wish is that men in the world below may sometimes pick up this tale when they are recovering from sleep or drunkenness, or when they wish to escape from business worries or a fit of the dumps, and in doing so find not only mental refreshment but even perhaps, if they will heed its lesson and abandon their vain and frivolous pursuits, some small arrest in the deterioration of their vital forces. What does your reverence say to that?'

For a long time Vanitas stood lost in thought, pondering this speech. He then subjected the *Story of the Stone* to a careful second reading. He could see that its main theme was love; that it consisted quite simply of a true record of real events; and that it was entirely free from any tendency to deprave and corrupt. He therefore copied it all out from beginning to end and took it back with him to look for a publisher.

As a consequence of all this, Vanitas, starting off in the Void (which is Truth) came to the contemplation of Form (which is Illusion); and from Form engendered Passion; and by communicating Passion, entered again into Form; and from Form awoke to the Void (which is Truth). He therefore changed his name from Vanitas to Brother Amor, or the Passionate Monk, (because he had approached Truth by way of Passion), and changed the title of the book from *The Story of the Stone* to *The Tale of Brother Amor*.

Old Kong Mei-xi from the homeland of Confucius

called the book *A Mirror for the Romantic*. Wu Yu-feng called it *A Dream of Golden Days*. Cao Xueqin in his Nostalgia Studio worked on it for ten years, in the course of which he rewrote it no less than five times, dividing it into chapters, composing chapter headings, renaming it *The Twelve Beauties of Jinling*, and adding an introductory quatrain. Red Inkstone restored the original title when he recopied the book and added his second set of annotations to it.

This, then, is a true account of how *The Story of the Stone* came to be written.

> Pages full of idle words
> Penned with hot and bitter tears:
> All men call the author fool;
> None his secret message hears.

The origin of *The Story of the Stone* has now been made clear. The same cannot, however, be said of the characters and events which it recorded. Gentle reader, have patience! This is how the inscription began:

Long, long ago the world was tilted downwards towards the south-east; and in that lower-lying south-easterly part of the earth there is a city called Soochow; and in Soochow the district around the Chang-men Gate is reckoned one of the two or three wealthiest and most fashionable quarters in the world of men. Outside the Chang-men Gate is a wide thoroughfare called Worldly Way; and somewhere off Worldly Way is an area called Carnal Lane. There is an old temple in the Carnal Lane area which, because of the way it is bottled up inside a narrow *cul-de-sac*, is referred to locally as Bottle-gourd Temple. Next door to Bottle-gourd Temple lived a gentleman of private means called Zhen Shi-yin and his wife Feng-shi, a kind, good woman with a profound sense of decency and decorum. The household was not a particularly wealthy one, but they were nevertheless looked up to by all and sundry as the leading family in the neighbourhood.

Zhen Shi-yin himself was by nature a quiet and totally unambitious person. He devoted his time to his garden and to the pleasures of wine and poetry. Except for a single flaw, his existence could, indeed, have been described as an idyllic one. The flaw was that, although already past fifty, he had no son, only a little girl, just two years old, whose name was Ying-lian.

Once, during the tedium of a burning summer's day,

Shi-yin was sitting idly in his study. The book had slipped from his nerveless grasp and his head had nodded down onto the desk in a doze. While in this drowsy state he seemed to drift off to some place he could not identify, where he became aware of a monk and a Taoist walking along and talking as they went.

'Where do you intend to take that thing you are carrying?' the Taoist was asking.

'Don't you worry about him!' replied the monk with a laugh. 'There is a batch of lovesick souls awaiting incarnation in the world below whose fate is due to be decided this very day. I intend to take advantage of this opportunity to slip our little friend in amongst them and let him have a taste of human life with the rest.'

'Well, well, so another lot of these amorous wretches is about to enter the vale of tears,' said the Taoist. 'How did all this begin? And where are the souls to be reborn?'

'You will laugh when I tell you,' said the monk. 'When this stone was left unused by the goddess, he found himself at a loose end and took to wandering about all over the place for want of better to do, until one day his wanderings took him to the place where the fairy Disenchantment lives.

w Disenchantment could tell that there was
thing unusual about this stone, so she kept him
re in her Sunset Glow Palace and gave him the hon-
orary title of Divine Luminescent Stone-in-Waiting in
the Court of Sunset Glow.

'But most of his time he spent west of Sunset Glow
exploring the banks of the Magic River. There, by the
Rock of Rebirth, he found the beautiful Crimson Pearl
Flower, for which he conceived such a fancy that he
took to watering her every day with sweet dew,
thereby conferring on her the gift of life.

'Crimson Pearl's substance was composed of the pur-
est cosmic essences, so she was already half-divine; and
now, thanks to the vitalizing effect of the sweet dew,
she was able to shed her vegetable shape and assume
the form of a girl.

'This fairy girl wandered about outside the Realm of
Separation, eating the Secret Passion Fruit when she
was hungry and drinking from the Pool of Sadness
when she was thirsty. The consciousness that she owed
the stone something for his kindness in watering her
began to prey on her mind and ended by becoming an
obsession.

' "I have no sweet dew here that I can repay him with," she would say to herself. "The only way in which I could perhaps repay him would be with the tears shed during the whole of a mortal lifetime if he and I were ever to be reborn as humans in the world below."

'Because of this strange affair, Disenchantment has got together a group of amorous young souls, of which Crimson Pearl is one, and intends to send them down into the world to take part in the great illusion of human life. And as today happens to be the day on which this stone is fated to go into the world too, I am taking him with me to Disenchantment's tribunal for the purpose of getting him registered and sent down to earth with the rest of these romantic creatures.'

'How very amusing!' said the Taoist. 'I have certainly never heard of a debt of tears before. Why shouldn't the two of us take advantage of this opportunity to go down into the world ourselves and save a few souls? It would be a work of merit.'

'That is exactly what I was thinking,' said the monk. 'Come with me to Disenchantment's palace to get this absurd creature cleared. Then, when this last batch of romantic idiots goes down, you and I can go down with them. At present about half have already been born. They await this last batch to make up the number.'

'Very good, I will go with you then,' said the Taoist. Shi-yin heard all this conversation quite clearly, and curiosity impelled him to go forward and greet the two reverend gentlemen. They returned his greeting and asked him what he wanted.

'It is not often that one has the opportunity of listening to a discussion of the operations of *karma* such as the one I have just been privileged to overhear,' said Shi-yin. 'Unfortunately I am a man of very limited understanding and have not been able to derive the full benefit from your conversation. If you would have the very great kindness to enlighten my benighted understanding with a somewhat fuller account of what you were discussing, I can promise you the most devout attention. I feel sure that your teaching would have a salutary effect on me and—who knows—might save me from the pains of hell.'

The reverend gentlemen laughed. 'These are heavenly mysteries and may not be divulged. But if you

14

wish to escape from the fiery pit, you have only to remember us when the time comes, and all will be well.'

Shi-yin saw that it would be useless to press them. 'Heavenly mysteries must not, of course, be revealed. But might one perhaps inquire what the "absurd creature" is that you were talking about? Is it possible that I might be allowed to see it?'

'Oh, as for that,' said the monk: 'I think it is on the cards for you to have a look at *him*,' and he took the object from his sleeve and handed it to Shi-yin.

Shi-yin took the object from him and saw that it was a clear, beautiful jade on one side of which were carved the words 'Magic Jade'. There were several columns of smaller characters on the back, which Shi-yin was just going to examine more closely when the monk, with a cry of 'Here we are, at the frontier of Illusion', snatched the stone from him and disappeared, with the Taoist, through a big stone archway above which

THE LAND OF ILLUSION

was written in large characters. A couplet in smaller characters was inscribed vertically on either side of the arch:

> Truth becomes fiction when the fiction's true;
> Real becomes not-real where the unreal's real.

Shi-yin was on the point of following them through the archway when suddenly a great clap of thunder seemed to shake the earth to its very foundations, making him cry out in alarm.

And there he was sitting in his study, the contents of his dream already half forgotten, with the sun still blazing on the ever-rustling plantains outside, and the wet-nurse at the door with his little daughter Ying-lian in her arms. Her delicate little pink-and-white face seemed dearer to him than ever at that moment, and he stretched out his arms to take her and hugged her to him.

After playing with her for a while at his desk, he carried her out to the front of the house to watch the bustle in the street. He was about to go in again when he saw a monk and a Taoist approaching, the monk scabby-headed and barefoot, the Taoist tousle-haired and limping. They were behaving like madmen, shouting with laughter and gesticulating wildly as they walked along.

When this strange pair reached Shi-yin's door and

saw him standing there holding Ying-lian, the monk burst into loud sobs. 'Patron,' he said, addressing Shi-yin, 'what are you doing, holding in your arms that ill-fated creature who is destined to involve both her parents in her own misfortune?'

Shi-yin realized that he was listening to the words of a madman and took no notice. But the monk persisted:

'Give her to me! Give her to me!'

Shi-yin was beginning to lose patience and, clasping his little girl more tightly to him, turned on his heel and was about to re-enter the house when the monk pointed his finger at him, roared with laughter, and then proceeded to intone the following verses:

> 'Fond man, your pampered child to cherish so—
> That caltrop-glass which shines on melting snow!
> Beware the high feast of the fifteenth day,
> When all in smoke and fire shall pass away!'

Shi-yin heard all this quite plainly and was a little worried by it. He was thinking of asking the monk what lay behind these puzzling words when he heard the Taoist say, 'We don't need to stay together. Why don't we part company here and each go about his own business? Three *kalpas* from now I shall wait for you on Bei-mang Hill. Having joined forces again there, we can go together to the Land of Illusion to sign off.'

'Excellent!' said the other. And the two of them went off and soon were both lost to sight.

'There must have been something behind all this,' thought Shi-yin to himself. 'I really ought to have asked him what he meant, but now it is too late.'

Jia Bao-yu visits the Land of Illusion
And the Fairy Disenchantment performs the
'Dream of Golden Days'

JIA BAO-YU, THE YOUNGEST SCION OF THE JIA CLAN,
WAS BORN WITH THE MYSTICAL PIECE OF JADE IN
HIS MOUTH.

The winter plum in the gardens of the Ning Mansion was now at its best, and this particular day Cousin Zhen's wife, You-shi, had some wine taken into the gardens and came over in person, bringing her son Jia Rong and his young wife with her, to invite Grandmother Jia, Lady Xing and Lady Wang to a flower-viewing party.

Grandmother Jia and the rest went round as soon as they had finished their breakfast. The party was in the All-scents Garden. It began with tea and continued with wine, and as it was a family gathering confined to the ladies of the Ning and Rong households, nothing particularly worth recording took place.

At one point in the party Bao-yu was overcome with

tiredness and heaviness and expressed a desire to take an afternoon nap. Grandmother Jia ordered some of the servants to go back to the house with him and get him comfortably settled, adding that they might return with him later when he was rested; but Qin-shi, the little wife of Jia Rong, smilingly proposed an alternative.

'We have got just the room here for Uncle Bao. Leave him to me, Grannie dear! He will be quite safe in my hands.'

She turned to address the nurses and maidservants who were in attendance on Bao-yu.

'Come, my dears! Tell Uncle Bao to follow me.'

Grandmother Jia had always had a high opinion of Qin-shi's trustworthiness—she was such a charming, delightful little creature, the favourite among her great-granddaughters-in-law—and was quite content to leave the arrangements to her.

Qin-shi conducted Bao-yu and his little knot of attendants to an inner room in the main building. As they entered, Bao-yu glanced up and saw a painting hanging above them on the opposite wall. The figures in it were very finely executed. They represented Scholarly Diligence in the person of the Han philosopher Liu Xiang at his book, obligingly illuminated for him by a supernatural being holding a large flaming torch. Bao-yu found the painting—or rather its subject—distasteful. But the pair of mottoes which flanked it proved the last straw:

> True learning implies a clear insight into human activities.
> Genuine culture involves the skilful manipulation of human relationships.

In vain the elegant beauty and splendid furnishings of the room! Qin-shi was given to understand in no uncertain terms that her uncle Bao-yu wished to be out of it *at once*.

'If this is not good enough for you,' said Qin-shi with a laugh, 'where *are* we going to put you?—unless you would like to have your rest in my bedroom.'

A little smile played over Bao-yu's face and he nodded. The nurses were shocked.

'An uncle sleep in the bedroom of his nephew's wife! Who ever heard of such a thing!'

Qin-shi laughed again.

'He won't misbehave. Good gracious, he's only a little boy! We don't have to worry about that sort of thing yet! You know my little brother who came last month: he's the same age as Uncle Bao, but if you stood them side by side I shouldn't be a bit surprised if he wasn't the taller of the two.'

'Why haven't I seen your brother yet?' Bao-yu demanded. 'Bring him in and let me have a look at him!'

The servants all laughed.

'Bring him in? Why, he's ten or twenty miles away! But I expect you'll meet him one of these days.'

In the course of this exchange the party had made its way to Qin-shi's bedroom. As Bao-yu entered, a subtle whiff of the most delicious perfume assailed his nostrils, making a sweet stickiness inside his drooping eyelids and causing all the joints in his body to dissolve.

'What a lovely smell!'

He repeated the words several times over.

Inside the room there was a painting by Tang Yin entitled 'Spring Slumber' depicting a beautiful woman asleep under a crab-apple tree, whose buds had not yet opened. The painting was flanked on either side by a pair of calligraphic scrolls inscribed with a couplet from the brush of the Song poet Qin Guan:

(on one side)

The coldness of spring has imprisoned the soft buds in
  a wintry dream;

(on the other side)

The fragrance of wine has intoxicated the beholder
  with imagined flower-scents.

On a table stood an antique mirror that had once
graced the tiring-room of the lascivious empress Wu
Ze-tian. Beside it stood the golden platter on which
Flying Swallow once danced for her emperor's delight.
And on the platter was that very quince which the vil-
lainous An Lu-shan threw at beautiful Yang Gui-fei,
bruising her plump white breast. At the far end of the
room stood the priceless bed on which Princess Shou-
yang was sleeping out of doors under the eaves of the
Han-zhang Palace when the plum-flower lighted on her
forehead and set a new fashion for coloured patches.
Over it hung a canopy commissioned by Princess
Tong-chang entirely fashioned out of ropes of pearls.

  'I like it here,' said Bao-yu happily.

  'My room,' said Qin-shi with a proud smile, 'is fit
for an immortal to sleep in.' And she unfolded a

quilted coverlet, whose silk had been laundered by the fabulous Xi Shi, and arranged the double head-rest that Hong-niang once carried for her amorous mistress.

The nurses now helped Bao-yu into bed and then tiptoed out, leaving him attended only by his four young maids: Aroma, Skybright, Musk, and Ripple. Qin-shi told them to go outside and stop the cats from fighting on the eaves.

As soon as Bao-yu closed his eyes he sank into a confused sleep in which Qin-shi was still there yet at the same time seemed to be drifting along weightlessly in front of him. He followed her until they came to a place of marble terraces and vermillion balustrades where there were green trees and crystal streams. Everything in this place was so clean and so pure that it seemed as if no human foot could ever have trodden there or floating speck of dust blown into it. Bao-yu's dreaming self rejoiced. 'What a delightful place!' he thought. 'If only I could spend all my life here! How much nicer it would be than living under the daily restraint of my parents and teachers!'

These idle reflections were interrupted by someone singing a song on the other side of a hill:

'Spring's dream-time will like drifting clouds disperse,
Its flowers snatched by a flood none can reverse.
Then tell each nymph and swain
'Tis folly to invite love's pain!'

It was the voice of a girl. Before its last echoes had
died away, a beautiful woman appeared in the quarter
from which the voice had come, approaching him with
a floating, fluttering motion. She was quite unlike any
earthly lady, as the following poem will make clear:

> She has left her willow-tree house, from her blos-
> soming bower stepped out;
> For the birds betray where she walks through the trees
> that cluster about,
> And a shadow athwart the winding walk announces
> that she is near,
> And a fragrance of musk and orchid from fluttering
> fairy sleeves,
> And a tinkle of girdle-gems that falls on the ear
> At each movement of her dress of lotus leaves.
> A peach-tree blossoms in her dimpling cheek;
> Her cloud-coiled tresses are halcyon-sleek;
> And she reveals, through parted cherry lips,
> Teeth like pomegranate pips.

Her slim waist's sinuous swaying calls to mind
The dance of snowflakes with the waltzing wind;
Hair ornaments of pearl and halcyon blue
Outshine her painted forehead's golden hue.
Her face, through blossoms fleetingly disclosed,
To mirth or ire seems equally disposed;
And as by the waterside she goes,
Hovering on light-stepping toes,
A half-incipient look of pique
Says she would speak, yet would not speak;
While her feet, with the same irresolution,
Would halt, yet would not interrupt their motion.
I contemplate her rare complexion,
Ice-pure and jade-like in perfection;
I marvel at her glittering dress,
Where art lends grace to sumptuousness;
I wonder at her fine-cut features—
Marble, which fragrance marks as one with living crea-
    tures;
And I admire her queenly gait,
Like stately dance of simurgh with his mate.
Her purity I can best show
In plum-trees flowering in the snow;
Her chastity I shall recall
In orchids white at first frost-fall;
Her tranquil nature will prevail,

Constant as lone pine in an empty vale;
Her loveliness as dazzled make
As sunset gilding a pellucid lake;
Her glittering elegance I can compare
With dragons in an ornamental mere;
Her dreamy soulfulness most seems
Like wintry waters in the moon's cold beams.
The beauties of days gone by by her beauty are all
    abashed.
Where was she born, and from whence descended?
Immortal I judge her, fresh come from fairy feastings
    by the Jasper Pool,
Or from fluting in starry halls, some heavenly concert
    ended.

Observing delightedly that the lady was a fairy,
Bao-yu hurried forward and saluted her with a smile.

'Madam Fairy, I don't know where you have come
from or where you are going to, but as I am quite lost
in this place, will you please take me with you and be
my guide?'

'I am the fairy Disenchantment,' the fairy woman replied. 'I live beyond the Realm of Separation, in the
Sea of Sadness. There is a Mountain of Spring Awakening which rises from the midst of that sea, and on

27

that mountain is the Paradise of the Full-blown Flower, and in that paradise is the Land of Illusion, which is my home. My business is with the romantic passions, love-debts, girlish heartbreaks and male philanderings of your dust-stained, human world. The reason I have come here today is that recently there has been a heavy concentration of love-*karma* in this area, and I hope to be able to find an opportunity of distributing a quantity of amorous thoughts by implanting them in the appropriate breasts. My meeting you here today is no accident but a part of the same project.

'This place where we are now is not so very far from my home. I have not much to offer you, but would you like to come back with me and let me try to entertain you? I have some fairy tea, which I picked myself. You could have a cup of that. And I have a few jars of choice new wine of my own brewing. I have also been rehearsing a fairy choir and a troupe of fairy dancers in a twelve-part suite which I recently composed called "A Dream of Golden Days". I could get them to perform it for you. What do you think?'

Bao-yu was so excited by this invitation that he quite forgot to wonder what had become of Qin-shi in his eagerness to accompany the fairy. As he followed her, a big stone archway suddenly loomed up in front of them on which

THE LAND OF ILLUSION

was written in large characters. A couplet in smaller characters was inscribed on either side of the arch:

> Truth becomes fiction when the fiction's true;
> Real becomes not-real when the unreal's real.

Having negotiated the archway, they presently came to the gateway of a palace. The following words were inscribed horizontally above the lintel:

SEAS OF PAIN AND SKIES OF PASSION

whilst the following words were inscribed vertically on the two sides:

> Ancient earth and sky
>   Marvel that love's passion should outlast all time.
> Star-crossed men and maids
>   Groan that love's debts should be so hard to pay.

'I see,' said Bao-yu to himself. 'I wonder what the meaning of "passion that outlasts all time" can be. And what are "love debts"? From now on I must make an effort to understand these things.'

He could not, of course, have known it, but merely by thinking this he had invited the attention of the demon Lust, and at that very moment a little of the demon's evil poison had entered Bao-yu's body and lodged itself in the innermost recesses of his heart.

Wholly unconscious of his mortal peril, Bao-yu continued to follow the fairy woman. They passed through a second gateway, and Bao-yu saw a range of palace buildings ahead of them on either hand. The entrance to each building had a board above it proclaiming its name, and there were couplets on either side of the doorway. Bao-yu did not have time to read all of the names, but he managed to make out a few, viz:

DEPARTMENT OF FOND INFATUATION
DEPARTMENT OF CRUEL REJECTION
DEPARTMENT OF EARLY MORNING WEEPING
DEPARTMENT OF LATE NIGHT SOBBING
DEPARTMENT OF SPRING FEVER
DEPARTMENT OF AUTUMN GRIEF

'Madam Fairy,' said Bao-yu, whose interest had been whetted by what he had managed to read, 'could you take me inside these offices to have a look around?'

'In these offices,' said the fairy woman, 'are kept registers in which are recorded the past, present and future of girls from all over the world. It is not permitted that your earthly eyes should look on things that are yet to come.'

Bao-yu was most unwilling to accept this answer, and begged and pleaded so persistently that at last Disenchantment gave in.

'Very well. You may make a very brief inspection of this office here.'

Delighted beyond measure, Bao-yu raised his head and read the notice above the doorway:

DEPARTMENT OF THE ILL FATED FAIR

The couplet inscribed vertically on either side of the doorway was as follows:

Spring griefs and autumn sorrows were by yourselves
    provoked.

Flower faces, moonlike beauty were to what end disclosed?

Bao-yu grasped enough of the meaning to be affected by its melancholy.

Passing inside, he saw a dozen or more large cupboards with paper strips pasted on their doors on
which were written the names of different provinces.
He was careful to look out for the one belonging to his
own area and presently found one on which the paper
strip said 'Jinling, Twelve Beauties of, Main Register'.
Bao-yu asked Disenchantment what this meant, and
she explained that it was a register of the twelve most
outstanding girls of his home province.

'People all say what a big place Jinling is,' said
Bao-yu. 'Surely there should be more than just twelve
names? Why, even in my own home, if you count the
servants, there must be altogether several hundred
girls.'

'Certainly there are a great many girls in the whole
province,' said Disenchantment with a smile, 'but only
the most important ones have been selected for recording in this register. The registers in the cupboards on

either side contain two other selections from the same area. But of the host of ordinary girls outside those three dozen we keep no records.'

Bao-yu glanced at the other two cupboards referred to by Disenchantment. One was labelled 'Jinling, Twelve Beauties of, Supplementary Register No. 1'; the other was labelled 'Jinling, Twelve Beauties of, Supplementary Register No. 2'. Stretching out his hand he opened the door of the second one, took out Supplementary Register No. 2, which was like a large album, and opened it at the first page.

It was a picture, but not of a person or a view. The whole page was covered with dark ink washes representing storm-clouds or fog, followed on the next page by a few lines of verse:

> Seldom the moon shines in a cloudless sky,
> And days of brightness all too soon pass by.
> A noble and aspiring mind
> In a base-born frame confined,
> Your charm and wit did only hatred gain,
> And in the end you were by slanders slain,
> Your gentle lord's solicitude in vain.

Bao-yu could not make much sense of this, and turned to the next page. It was another picture, this time of a bunch of fresh flowers and a worn-out mat, again followed by a few lines of verse.

What price your kindness and compliance,
Of sweetest flower the rich perfume?
You chose the player fortune favoured,
Unmindful of your master's doom.

Bao-yu was even more mystified by this than by the first page, and laying the album aside, opened the door of the cupboard marked 'Supplementary Register No. 1' and took out the album from that.

As in the previous album, the first page was a picture. It represented a branch of cassia with a pool underneath. The water in the pool had dried up and the mud in the bottom was dry and cracked. Growing from it was a withered and broken lotus plant. The picture was followed by these lines:

Your stem grew from a noble lotus root,
Yet your life passed, poor flower, in low repute.

The day two earths shall bear a single tree,
Your soul must fly home to its own country.

Once more failing to make any sense of what he saw, Bao-yu picked up the Main Register to look at. In this album the picture on the first page represented two dead trees with a jade belt hanging in their branches and on the ground beneath them a pile of snow in which a golden hairpin lay half-buried. This was followed by a quatrain:

One was a pattern of female virtue,
One a wit who made other wits seem slow.
The jade belt in the greenwood hangs,
The gold pin is buried beneath the snow.

Still Bao-yu was unable to understand the meaning. He would have liked to ask, but he knew Disenchantment would be unwilling to divulge the secrets of her immortal world. Yet though he could make no sense of the book, for some reason he found himself unable this time to lay it down, and continued to look through it to the end.

The picture that followed was of a bow with a citron hanging from it, followed by what looked like the words of a song:

> You shall, when twenty years in life's hard school are
>   done,
> In pomegranate-time to palace halls ascend.
> Though three springs never could with your first spring
>   compare,
> When hare meets tiger your great dream shall end.

Next was a picture of two people flying a kite. There was also a large expanse of sea with a boat in it and a girl in the boat who had buried her face in her hands and appeared to be crying. This was followed by a quatrain:

> Blessed with a shrewd mind and a noble heart,
> Yet born in time of twilight and decay,
> In spring through tears at river's bank you gaze,
> Borne by the wind a thousand miles away.

The next picture showed some scudding wisps of cloud and a stretch of running water followed by these words:

What shall avail you rank and riches,
Orphaned while yet in swaddling bands you lay?
Soon you must mourn your bright sun's early setting.
The Xiang flows and the Chu clouds sail away.

Next was a picture showing a beautiful jade which
had fallen into the mud, followed by words of judgement:

> For all your would-be spotlessness
> And vaunted otherworldliness,
> You that look down on common flesh and blood,
> Yourself impure, shall end up in the mud.

Next was a striking picture of a savage wolf pursu-
ing a beautiful girl. He had just seized her with his
jaws and appeared to be about to ear her. Underneath
it was written:

> Paired with a brute like the wolf in the old fable,
> Who on his saviour turned when he was able,
> To cruelty not used, your gentle heart
> Shall, in a twelvemonth only, break apart.

After this was an old temple with a beautiful girl sitting all on her own inside it reading a Buddhist sūtra. The words said:

When you see through the spring scene's transient state,
A nun's black habit shall replace your own.
Alas, that daughter of so great a house
By Buddha's altar lamp should sleep alone!

Next was an iceberg with a hen phoenix perched on the top of it, and these words:

This phoenix in a bad time came;
All praised her great ability.
'Two' makes my riddle with a man and tree:
Returning south in tears she met calamity.

Next was a cottage in a deserted village inside which a beautiful girl sat spinning, followed by these words:

When power is lost, rank matters not a jot;
When families fall, kinship must be forgot.
Through a chance kindness to a country wife
Deliverance came for your afflicted life.

This was followed by a picture of a vigorously growing orchid in a pot, beside which stood a lady in full
court dress. The words said:

> The plum-tree bore her fruit after the rest,
> Yet, when all's done, her Orchid was the best.
> Against your ice-pure nature all in vain
> The tongues of envy wagged; you felt no pain.

The picture after that showed an upper room in a
tall building in which a beautiful girl was hanging by
her neck from a beam, having apparently taken her
own life. The words said:

> Love was her sea, her sky; in such excess
> Love, meeting with its like, breeds wantonness.
> Say not our troubles all from Rong's side came;
> For their beginning Ning must take the blame.

Bao-yu would have liked to see some more, but the
fairy woman, knowing how intelligent and sharp-
witted he was, began to fear that she was in danger of
becoming responsible for a leakage of celestial secrets,
and so, snapping the album shut, she said with a

laugh, 'Come with me and we will do some more sight-seeing. Why stay here puzzling your head over these silly riddles?'

Next moment, without quite knowing how it happened, Bao-yu found that he had left the place of registers behind him and was following Disenchantment through the rear parts of the palace. Everywhere there were buildings with ornately carved and painted eaves and rafters, their doorways curtained with strings of pearls and their interiors draped with embroidered hangings. The courtyards outside them were full of deliciously fragrant fairy blooms and rare aromatic herbs.

Gleam of gold pavement flashed on scarlet doors,
And in jade walls jewelled casements snow white shone.

'Hurry, hurry! Come out and welcome the honoured guest!' he heard Disenchantment calling to someone inside, and almost at once a bevy of fairy maidens came running from the palace, lotus sleeves fluttering and feather-skirts billowing, each as enchantingly beautiful as the flowers of spring or the autumn moon. Seeing

Bao-yu, they began to reproach Disenchantment angrily.

'So this is your "honoured guest"! What do you mean by making us hurry out to meet *him*? You told us that today at this very hour the dream-soul of our darling Crimson Pearl was coming to play with us, and we have been waiting I don't know how long for her arrival. And now, instead, you have brought this disgusting creature to pollute our pure, maidenly precincts. What's the idea?'

At these words Bao-yu was suddenly overwhelmed with a sense of the uncleanness and impurity of his own body and sought in vain for somewhere to escape to; but Disenchantment held him by the hand and advanced towards the fairy maidens with a conciliatory smile.

'Let me tell you the reason for my change of plan. It is true that I set off for the Rong mansion with the intention of fetching Crimson Pearl, but as I was passing through the Ning mansion on my way, I happened to run into the Duke of Ning-guo and his brother the Duke of Rong-guo and they laid a solemn charge on me which I found it hard to refuse.

' "In the hundred years since the foundation of the

present dynasty," they said, "several generations of our house have distinguished themselves by their services to the Throne and have covered themselves with riches and honours; but now its stock of good fortune has run out, and nothing can be done to replenish it. And though our descendants are many, not one of them is worthy to carry on the line. The only possible exception, our great-grandson Bao-yu, has inherited a perverse, intractable nature and is eccentric and emotionally unstable; and although his natural brightness and intelligence augur well, we fear that owing to the fated eclipse of our family's fortunes there will be no one at hand to give the lad proper guidance and to start him along the right lines.

' "May we profit from the fortunate accident of this encounter, Madam, to entreat you to take the boy in hand for us? Could you perhaps initiate him in the pleasures of the flesh and all that sort of thing in such a way as to shock the silliness out of him? In that way he might stand a chance of escaping some of the traps that people fall into and be able to devote himself single-mindedly to the serious things of life. It would be such a kindness if you would do this for us."

'Hearing the old gentlemen so earnest in their entreaty, I was moved to compassion and agreed to bring the boy here. I began by letting him have a good look at the records of the three grades of girls belonging to his own household; but the experience did not bring any awareness; and so I have brought him to this place for another attempt. It is my hope that a full exposure to the illusions of feasting, drinking, music and dancing may succeed in bringing about an awakening in him some time in the future.'

Having concluded her explanation, she led Bao-yu indoors. At once he became aware of a faint, subtle scent, the source of which he was quite unable to identify and about which he felt impelled to question Disenchantment.

'How could you possibly know what it was,' said Disenchantment with a somewhat scornful smile, 'since this perfume is not to be found anywhere in your mortal world? It is made from the essences of rare plants found on famous mountains and other places of great natural beauty, culled when they are new-grown and blended with gums from the pearl-laden trees that grow in the jewelled groves of paradise. It is called "Belles Se Fanent".'

Bao-yu expressed his admiration.

The company now seated themselves, and some little maids served them with tea. Bao-yu found its fragrance fresh and clean and its flavour delicious, totally unlike those of any earthly blend he knew. He asked Disenchantment for the name.

'The leaves are picked in the Paradise of the Full-blown Flower on the Mountain of Spring Awakening,' Disenchantment informed him. 'It is infused in water collected from the dew that lies on fairy flowers and leaves. The name is "Maiden's Tears".'

Bao-yu nodded attentively and commended the tea. Looking around the room he noticed various musical instruments, antique bronzes, paintings by old masters, poems by new poets, and other hallmarks of gracious living. He was particularly delighted to observe some rouge-stained pieces of cotton-wool lying on the window-sill—evidently the aftermath of some fairy-woman's toilet. A pair of calligraphic scrolls hung on the wall, making up the following couplet:

Earth's choicest spirits in the dark lie hid:
Heaven ineluctably enforced their fate.

After reading the scrolls, Bao-yu asked to be introduced to the fairy maidens. They had a strange assortment of names. One was called Dream-of-bliss, another was called Loving-heart, a third Ask-for-trouble, a fourth Past-regrets, and the rest all had names that were equally bizarre.

Presently the little maids came in again and proceeded to arrange some chairs around a table and to lay it with food and wine for a feast. In the words of the poet,

> Celestial nectar filled the crystal cup,
> And liquid gold in amber goblets glowed.

The wine's bouquet was delectable, and once again Bao-yu could not resist asking about it.

'This wine,' said Disenchantment, 'is made from the petals of hundreds of different kinds of flowers and extracts from thousands of different sorts of trees. These are blended and fermented with kylin's marrow and phoenix milk. Hence its name, *"Lachrymae Rerum"*.'

Bao-yu praised it enthusiastically.

As they sat drinking wine, a troupe of twelve dancers entered and inquired what pieces they should perform for the company's entertainment.

'You can do the twelve songs of my new song-and-dance suite "A Dream of Golden Days",' said Disenchantment.

At once the sandalwood clappers began, very softly, to beat out a rhythm, accompanied by the sedate twang of the *zheng*'s silver strings and by the voice of a singer.

'When first the world from chaos rose . . .'

The singer had got no further than the first line of the first song when Disenchantment interrupted.

'This suite,' she told Bao-yu, 'is not like the music-dramas of your earthly composers in which there are always the fixed parts of *sheng, dan, jing, mo* and so on, and set tunes in the various Northern and Southern modes. In my suite each song is an elegy on a single person or event and the tunes are original compositions which we have orchestrated ourselves. You need to know what the songs are about in order to appreciate them properly. I should not imagine you are very familiar with this sort of entertainment; so unless you read the libretto of the songs first before listening to them, I fear you may find them rather insipid.'

Turning to one of the maids, she ordered her to fetch the manuscript of her libretto of 'A Dream of Golden Days' and gave it to Bao-yu to read, so that he could listen to the songs with one eye on the text. These were the words in Disenchantment's manuscript:

Prelude: *A Dream of Golden Days*

When first the world from chaos rose,
Tell me, how did love begin?
The wind and moonlight first did love compose.
Now woebegone
And quite cast down
In low estate
I would my foolish heart expose,
And so perform
This *Dream of Golden Days*,
And all my grief for my lost loves disclose.

First Song: *The Mistaken Marriage*

Let others all
Commend the marriage rites of gold and jade;

I still recall
The bond of old by stone and flower made;
And while my vacant eyes behold
Crystalline snows of beauty pure and cold,
From my mind can not be banished
That fairy wood forlorn that from the world has vanished.
How true I find
That every good some imperfection holds!
Even a wife so courteous and so kind
No comfort brings to my afflicted mind.

Second Song: *Hope Betrayed*

One was a flower from paradise,
One a pure jade without spot or stain.
If each for the other one was not intended,
Then why in this life did they meet again?
And yet if fate had meant them for each other,
Why was their earthly meeting all in vain?
In vain were all her sighs and tears,
In vain were all his anxious fears:
All, insubstantial, doomed to pass,
As moonlight mirrored in the water
Or flowers reflected in a glass.
How many tears from those poor eyes could flow,
Which every season rained upon her woe?

Third Song: *Mutability*

In the full flower of her prosperity
Once more came mortal mutability,
Bidding her, with both eyes wide,
All earthly things to cast aside,
And her sweet soul upon the airs to glide.
So far the road back home did seem
That to her parents in a dream
Thus she her final duty paid:
'I that now am but a shade,
Parents dear,
For your happiness I fear:
Do not tempt the hand of fate!
Draw back, draw back, before it is too late!'

Fourth Song: *From Dear Ones Parted*

Sail, boat, a thousand miles through rain and wind,
Leaving my home and dear ones far behind.
I fear that my remaining years
Will waste away in homesick tears.
Father dear and mother mild,
Be not troubled for your child!
From of old our rising, falling
Was ordained; so now this parting.

Each in another land must be;
Each for himself must fend as best he may;
Now I am gone, oh do not weep for me!

Fifth Song: *Grief Amidst Gladness*

While you still in cradle lay,
Both your parents passed away.
Though born to silken luxury,
No warmth or kind indulgence came your way.
Yet yours was a generous, open-hearted nature,
And never could be snared or soured
By childish piques and envious passions—
You were a crystal house by wind and moonlight scoured.
Matched to a perfect, gentle husband,
Security of bliss at last it seemed,
And all your childish miseries redeemed.
But soon alas! the clouds of Gao-tang faded,
The waters of the Xiang ran dry.
In our grey world so are things always ordered:
What then avails it to lament and sigh?

Sixth Song: *All at Odds*

Heaven made you like a flower,
With grace and wit to match the gods,
Adding a strange, contrary nature
That set you with the rest at odds.
Nauseous to you the world's rank diet,
Vulgar its fashion's gaudy dress:
But the world envies the superior
And hates a too precious daintiness.
Sad it seemed that your life should in dim-lit shrines be
    wasted,
All the sweets of spring untasted:
Yet, at the last,
Down into mud and shame your hopes were cast,
Like a white, flawless jade dropped in the muck,
Where only wealthy rakes might bless their luck.

Seventh Song: *Husband and Enemy*

Zhong-shan wolf,
Inhuman sot,
Who for past kindnesses cared not a jot!
Bully and spendthrift, reckless in debauch,
For riot or for whoring always hot!
A delicate young wife of gentle stock

To you was no more than a lifeless block,
And bore, when you would rant and rave,
Treatment far worse than any slave;
So that her delicate, sweet soul
In just a twelvemonth from its body stole.

Eighth Song: *The Vanity of Spring*

When triple spring as vanity was seen,
What use the blushing flowers, the willows green?
From youth's extravagance you sought release.
To win chaste quietness and heavenly peace.
The hymeneal peach-blooms in the sky,
The flowering almond's blossoms seen on high
Dismiss, since none, for sure,
Can autumn's blighting frost endure.
Amidst sad aspens mourners sob and sigh,
In maple woods the poor ghosts thinly cry,
And under the dead grasslands lost graves lie.
Now poor, now rich, men's lives in toil are passed
To be, like summer's pride, cut down at last.
The doors of life and death all must go through.
Yet this I know is true:
In Paradise there grows a precious tree
Which bears the fruit of immortality.

Ninth Song: *Caught by Her Own Cunning*

Too shrewd by half, with such finesse you wrought
That your own life in your own toils was caught;
But long before you died your heart was slain,
And when you died your spirit walked in vain.
Fall'n the great house once so secure in wealth,
Each scattered member shifting for himself;
And half a life-time's anxious schemes
Proved no more than the stuff of dreams.
Like a great building's tottering crash,
Like flickering lampwick burned to ash,
Your scene of happiness concludes in grief:
For worldly bliss is always insecure and brief.

Tenth Song: *The Survivor*

Some good remained,
Some good remained:
The daughter found a friend in need
Through her mother's one good deed.
So let all men the poor and meek sustain,
And from the example of her cruel kin refrain,
Who kinship scorned and only thought of gain.
For far above the constellations
One watches all and makes just calculations.

Eleventh Song: *Splendour Come Late*

Favour, a shadow in the glass;
Fame, a dream that soon would pass:
The blissful flowering-time of youth soon fled,
Soon, too, the pleasures of the bridal bed.
A pearl-encrusted crown and robes of state
Could not for death untimely compensate;
And though each man desires
Old age from want made free,
True blessedness requires
A clutch of young heirs at the knee.
Proudly upright
The head with cap and bands of office on,
And gleaming bright
Upon his breast the gold insignia shone.
An awesome sight
To see him so exalted stand!—
Yet the black night
Of death's dark frontier lay close at hand.
All those whom history calls great
Left only empty names for us to venerate.

Twelfth Song: *The Good Things Have an End*

Perfumed was the dust that fell
From painted beams where springtime ended.
Her sportive heart
And amorous looks
The ruin of a mighty house portended.
The weakness in the line began with Jing;
The blame for the decline lay first in Ning;
But retribution all was of Love's fashioning.

Epliogue: *The Birds into the Wood Have Flown*

The office jack's career is blighted,
The rich man's fortune now all vanished,
The kind with life have been requited,
The cruel exemplarily punished;
The one who owed a life is dead,
The tears one owed have all been shed.
Wrongs suffered have the wrongs done expiated;
The couplings and the sunderings were fated.
Untimely death sin in some past life shows,
But only luck a blest old age bestows.
The disillusioned to their convents fly,
The still deluded miserably die.

Like birds who, having fed, to the woods repair,
They leave the landscape desolate and bare.

Having reached the end of this suite, the singers showed signs of embarking on another one. Disenchantment observed with a sigh that Bao-yu was dreadfully bored.

'Silly boy! You still don't understand, do you?'

Bao-yu hurriedly stopped the girls and told them that they need not sing any more. He felt dizzy and his head was spinning. He explained to Disenchantment that he had drunk too much and would like to lie down.

At once she ordered the remains of the feasts to be removed and conducted Bao-yu to a dainty bedroom. The furnishings and hangings of the bed were more sumptuous and beautiful than anything he had ever seen. To his intense surprise there was a fairy girl sitting in the middle of it. Her rose-fresh beauty reminded him strongly of Bao-chai, but there was also something about her of Dai-yu's delicate charm. As he was pondering the meaning of this apparition, he suddenly became aware that Disenchantment was addressing him.

'In the rich and noble households of your mortal

world, too many of those bowers and boudoirs where innocent tenderness and sweet girlish fantasy should reign are injuriously defiled by coarse young voluptuaries and loose, wanton girls. And what is even more detestable, there are always any number of worthless philanderers to protest that it is woman's beauty alone that inspires them, or loving feelings alone, unsullied by any taint of lust. They lie in their teeth! To be moved by woman's beauty is itself a kind of lust. To experience loving feelings is, even more assuredly, a kind of lust. Every act of love, every carnal congress of the sexes is brought about precisely because sensual delight in beauty has kindled the feeling of love.

'The reason I like you so much is because you are full of lust. You are the most lustful person I have ever known in the whole world!'

Bao-yu was scared by the vehemence of her words.

'Madam Fairy, you are wrong! Because I am lazy over my lessons, Mother and Father still have to scold me quite often; but surely that doesn't make me *lustful*? I'm still too young to know what they do, the people they use that word about.'

'Ah, but you *are* lustful!' said Disenchantment. 'In principle, of course, all lust is the same. But the word has many different meanings. For example, the typically lustful man in the common sense of the word is a man who likes a pretty face, who is fond of singing and dancing, who is inordinately given to flirtation; one who makes love in season and out of season, and who, if he could, would like to have every pretty girl in the world at his disposal, to gratify his desires whenever he felt like it. Such a person is a mere brute. His is a shallow, promiscuous kind of lust.

'But your kind of lust is different. That blind, defenceless love with which nature has filled your being is what we call here "lust of the mind". "Lust of the mind" cannot be explained in words, nor, if it could, would you be able to grasp their meaning. Either you know what it means or your don't.

'Because of this "lust of the mind" women will find you a kind and understanding friend; but in the eyes of the world I am afraid it is going to make you seem unpractical and eccentric. It is going to earn you the jeers of many and the angry looks of many more.

'Today I received a most touching request on your behalf from your ancestors the Duke of Ning-guo and the Duke of Rong-guo. And as I cannot bear the idea of your being rejected by the world for the greater glory of us women, I have brought you here. I have made you drunk with fairy wine. I have drenched you with fairy tea. I have admonished you with fairy songs. And now I am going to give you my little sister Two-in-one—"Ke-qing" to her friends—to be your bride.

'The time is propitious. You may consummate the marriage this very night. My motive in arranging this is to help you grasp the fact that, since even in these immortal precincts love is an illusion, the love of your dust-stained, mortal world must be doubly an illusion. It is my earnest hope that, knowing this, you will henceforth be able to shake yourself free of its entanglements and change your previous way of thinking, devoting your mind seriously to the teachings of Confucius and Mencius and your person wholeheartedly to the betterment of society.'

Disenchantment then proceeded to give him secret instruction in the art of love; then, pushing him gently inside the room, she closed the door after him and went away.

Dazed and confused, Bao-yu nevertheless proceeded to follow out the instructions that Disenchantment had given him, which led him by predictable stages to that act which boys and girls perform together—and which it is not my intention to give a full account of here.

Next morning he lay for a long time locked in blissful tenderness with Ke-qing, murmuring sweet endearments in her ear and unable to tear himself away from her. Eventually they emerged from the bedroom hand in hand to walk together out-of-doors.

Their walk seemed to take them quite suddenly to a place where only thorn-trees grew and wolves and tigers prowled around in pairs. Ahead of them the road ended at the edge of a dark ravine. No bridge connected it with the other side. As they hesitated, wondering what to do, they suddenly became aware that Disenchantment was running up behind them.

'Stop! Stop!' she was shouting. 'Turn back at once! Turn back!'

Bao-yu stood still in alarm and asked her what place this was.

'This is the Ford of Error,' said Disenchantment. 'It is ten thousand fathoms deep and extends hundreds of miles in either direction. No boat can ever cross it; only a raft manned by a lay-brother called Numb and an acolyte called Dumb. Numb holds the steering-paddle and Dumb wields the pole. They won't ferry anyone across for money, but only take those who are fated to cross over.

'If you had gone on walking just now and had fallen in, all the good advice I was at such pains to give you would have been wasted!'

Even as she spoke there was a rumbling like thunder from inside the abyss and a multitude of demons and water monsters reached up and clutched Bao-yu to drag him down into its depths. In his terror the sweat broke out over his body like rain and a great cry burst from his lips,

'Ke-qing! Save me!'

Aroma and his other maids rushed upstairs in alarm and clung to him.

'Don't be frightened, Bao-yu! We are here!'

But Qin-shi, who was out in the courtyard telling the maids to be sure that the cats and dogs didn't fight, marvelled to hear him call her name out in his sleep.

' "Ke-qing" was the name they called me back at home when I was a little girl. Nobody here knows it. I wonder how he could have found it out?'

If you have not yet fathomed the answer to her question, you must read the next chapter.

A pupil is abused and
Tealeaf throws the classroom
in an uproar

QIN ZHONG, THE LITTLE BROTHER OF QIN SHI, HAS
BECOME CLOSE FRIENDS WITH JIA BAO-YU, AND
THEIR FAMILIES HAVE DECIDED THEY WILL GO TO
SCHOOL TOGETHER.

The Jia clan school was situated at no great distance
from Rong-guo House. It was a charitable foundation
which had been established many years previously by
the founder of the family and was designed for the
sons and younger brothers of those family members of
the clan who could not afford to pay for private tu-
ition. All members of the clan holding official posts
were expected to contribute towards its expenses and
members of advanced years and known integrity were
chosen to be its masters. As soon as Bao-yu and Qin
Zhong arrived they were introduced to the other stu-
dents and then set to work at once on their lessons.

From now on the two friends were inseparable, arriving at school and leaving school together and sitting beside each other in class. Grandmother Jia herself became very fond of Qin Zhong. She was always having him to stay for three or four nights at a time and treated him exactly as if he were one of her own great-grandchildren. And because she realized that his family was not very well off, she frequently helped out with clothes and the like. Within a month or two he was a familiar and accepted member of the Rong household.

Bao-yu had always been impatient of social conventions, preferring to let sentiment rather than convention dictate the terms of his relationships. It was this which now prompted him to make Qin Zhong the following proposal:

'You and I are schoolmates and pretty much the same age. Let us in future forget all this "uncle" "nephew" business and address each other exactly like friends or brothers!'

Qin Zhong was at first too timid to comply; but as Bao-yu persisted and went on calling him 'brother' or 'Jing-qing' (which was his school-name) whenever he spoke to him, Qin Zhong himself gradually fell into the habit of addressing Bao-yu as an equal.

All the pupils at the clan school were either members

of the Jia clan or relations by marriage; but as the proverb rightly says, 'there are nine kinds of dragon and no two kinds are alike'. Where many are gathered together the wheat is sure to contain a certain amount of chaff; and this school was no exception in numbering some very ill-bred persons among its pupils.

The two new boys, Qin Zhong and Bao-yu, were both as beautiful as flowers; the other scholars observed how shrinking and gentle Qin Zhong was, blushing almost before you spoke to him and timid and bashful as a girl; they saw in Bao-yu one whom nature and habit had made humble and accommodating in spite of his social position, always willing to defer to others in the interest of harmony; they observed his affectionate disposition and familiar manner of speech; and they could see that the two friends were devoted to each other. Perhaps it is not to be wondered at that these observations should have given rise to certain suspicions in the minds of those ill-bred persons, and that both in school and out of it all kinds of ugly rumours should have circulated behind their backs.

When Xue Pan learned, some time after moving into his aunt's place in the capital, that the establishment included a clan school plentifully stocked with young males of a certain age, his old enthusiasm for 'Lord Long-yang's vice' was reawakened, and he had hastened to register himself as a pupil. His school-going was, needless to say, a pretence—'one day fishing and two days to dry the nets' as they say—and had nothing to do with the advancement of learning. Having paid a generous fee to Jia Dai-ru, he used his membership of the school merely as a means of picking up 'soul-mates' from among his fellow-students. It must with regret be recorded that a surprisingly large number of the latter were deluded into becoming his willing victims by the prospect of receiving those ample advances of money and goods which he was in a position to offer.

Among them were two amorous young creatures whose names and parentage escape us but who, because of their glamorous looks and affected manners, were universally known by the nicknames of 'Darling' and 'Precious'. Although their fellow-students much admired them and entertained towards them feelings not at all conducive to that health of mind which the Young Person should at all times endeavour to cultivate, they were deterred from meddling with them for fear of what Xue Pan might do.

When Qin Zhong and Bao-yu joined the school it was only to be expected that they too should fall under the spell of this charming pair; but like the rest they were inhibited from overt declaration of their feelings by the knowledge that Xue Pan was their 'friend'. Their feelings were reciprocated by Darling and Precious, and a bond of mutual attraction grew up between the four, which nevertheless remained unexpressed, except for the significant looks that every day passed between them across the classroom, or the occasional rather too loud utterance to a neighbour of some remark really intended for the ears of the opposite pair.

They were persuaded that these cryptic communications had escaped the notice of their fellows; but they were wrong. Certain young hooligans among their classmates had long since discerned the true nature of what was going on, and while the two handsome couples were engaged in their silent and (as they thought) secret communion, these others would be winking and leering behind their backs or becoming suddenly convulsed with paroxysms of artificial coughing.

It happened that one day Jia Dai-ru was called home on business and left the class with the first half of a fourteen word couplet to complete, telling them that he would be back on the morrow to take them over the next passage in their reading and putting his eldest grandson Jia Rui in charge of the school during his absence. Xue Pan had by now stopped coming in even for roll-call, and so on this occasion he was out of the way. The opportunity was too good to miss, and Qin Zhong and Darling, after a preliminary exchange of glances, both asked to be excused and went round to the rear courtyard to converse.

'Does your father mind what friends you have?' Qin Zhong had got no further than this question when there was a cough behind them. The two boys spun round and saw that it came from their classmate 'Jokey' Jin. Darling had a somewhat impetuous nature which now, fired by a mixture of anger and shame, caused him to round sharply on the intruder.

'What's that cough supposed to mean? Aren't we allowed to talk if we want to?'

Jokey Jin leered: 'If you're allowed to talk, aren't I allowed to cough if I want to? What I'd like to know is, if you've got something to say to each other, why can't you say it out openly? Why all this guilty secrecy? But what's the good of pretending? It's a fair cop. You

68

let me in on your game and I won't say anything. Otherwise there'll be trouble!'

With furious blushes the other two protested indignantly that they did not know what he was talking about.

Jokey Jin grinned. 'Caught you in the act, didn't I?' He began to clap his hands and chant in a loud, guffawing voice,

> 'Bum-cake!
> Bum-cake!
> Let's all have a
> Bit to eat!'

Angry and indignant, Qin Zhong, and Darling hurried back into the classroom and complained to Jia Rui that Jokey Jin was persecuting them.

This Jia Rui was a spineless, unprincipled character who, as a means of obliging the boys to treat him, always displayed the most shameless favouritism in his settlement of classroom disputes. In return for money, drinks, and dinners, he had lately given Xue Pan a free hand in his nefarious activities—had, indeed, not only refrained from interfering with him, but even 'aided the tyrant in his tyranny'.

Now Xue Pan was very inconstant in his affections, always blowing east one day and west the next. He had recently abandoned Darling and Precious in favour of some newly discovered sweetheart, just as previously he had abandoned Jokey Jin in favour of Darling and Precious. It followed that in this present confrontation Jia Rui, to his chagrin, could not hope to gain any rewards by the exercise of his usual partiality. Instead of blaming this vexatious state of affairs on Xue Pan's fickleness, however, he directed all his resentment against Darling and Precious, for whom he felt the same unreasonable jealousy as motivated Jokey Jin and the rest.

Qin Zhong's and Darling's complaint at first put Jia Rui in somewhat of a quandary, for he dared not openly rebuke Qin Zhong. He could, however, give his resentment outlet by making an example of Darling; so instead of dealing with his complaint, he told him that he was a trouble-maker and followed this up with so savage a dressing-down that even Qin Zhong went back to his seat humiliated and crestfallen.

Jokey Jin, now thoroughly cock-a-hoop, wagged his

head and tutted in a most provoking manner and addressed wounding remarks to no one in particular, which greatly upset Darling and Precious for whose ears they were intended. A furious muttered altercation broke out between them across the intervening desks. Jokey Jin insisted that he had caught Qin Zhong and Darling *in flagrante delicto*.

'I ran into them in the back courtyard, kissing each other and feeling arses as plain as anything. I tell you they had it all worked out. They were just measuring themselves for size before getting down to business.'

Reckless in his hour of triumph, he made these wild allegations, unmindful of who might hear them. But one heroic soul was moved to mighty anger by his wanton words. This was Jia Qiang, a member of the Ning-guo branch of the family of the same generation as Jia Rong. He had lost both his parents when a small child and been brought up by Cousin Zhen. At sixteen he was even more handsome and dashing than Jia Rong and the two youths were inseparable friends.

Any establishment as large as the Ning household always contains a few disgruntled domestics who specialize in traducing their masters, and a number of disagreeable rumours concerning Jia Qiang did in fact begin to circulate among the servants which seem to have reached the ears of Cousin Zhen, for, partly in self-defence (since they involved him too), he moved Jia Qiang out of the house and set him up in a small establishment of his own somewhere in the city.

Jia Qiang possessed a very shrewd brain under his dazzlingly handsome exterior. His attendance at the school, however, was no more than a blind to his other activities, principal among which were cock-fighting, dog-racing, and botanizing excursions into the Garden of Pleasure; but with a doting Cousin Zhen to protect him on the one hand and Jia Rong to aid and comfort him on the other, there was no one in the clan who dared thwart him in anything he did.

Since Qin Zhong was the brother-in-law of his best friend, Jia Qiang was naturally unwilling to stand by and see him abused in so despiteful a manner without doing anything to help. On the other hand he reflected that there would be certain disadvantages in coming forward as his champion.

'Jokey Jin, Jia Rui, and that lot are friends of Uncle Xue,' he thought. 'For that matter, I'm a friend of Uncle Xue myself. If I openly stick up for Qin Zhong and they go and tell old Xue, it'll make things rather awk-

ward between us. On the other hand, if I don't inter-
fere at all, Jokey Jin's rumours are going to get quite
out of hand. This calls for a stratagem of some kind
which will shut the little beast up without causing too
much embarrassment afterwards.'

Having thought of a plan, he pretended that he
wanted to be excused, and slipping round to the back,
quietly called over Bao-yu's little page Tealeaf and
whispered a few inflammatory words in his ear.

Tealeaf was the most willing but also the youngest
and least sensible of Bao-yu's pages. Jia Qiang told him
how Jokey Jin had been bullying Qin Zhong. 'And
even Bao-yu came in for a share,' he said. 'If we don't
take this Jin fellow down a peg, next time he is going
to be quite insufferable.'

Tealeaf never needed any encouragement to pick a
fight, and now, inflamed by Jia Qiang's message and
open incitement to action, he marched straight into the
classroom to look for Jokey Jin. And there was no
'Master Jin' when he saw him, either: it was 'Jin! Who
do you think you are?'

At this point Jia Qiang began to scrape his boots on
the floor and make a great business of straightening his
clothes and glancing out of the window at the sky,

muttering to himself as he did so, 'Ah, yes. Hmn. Must be about time.' Going up to Jia Rui, he informed him that he had an engagement which necessitated his leaving early, and Jia Rui, not having the courage to stop him, allowed him to slip away.

Tealeaf had by now singled out Jokey Jin and grabbed him by the front of his jacket.

'Whether we fuck arseholes or not,' he said, 'what fucking business is it of yours? You should be bloody grateful we haven't fucked your dad. Come outside and fight it out with me, if you've got any spunk in you!'

'Tealeaf!' Jia Rui shouted agitatedly. 'You are not to use such language in here!'

Jokey Jin's face turned pale with anger.

'This is mutiny! I don't have to take this sort of thing from a slave. I shall see your master about this'— and he shook himself free of Tealeaf and made for Bao-yu, intending to seize and belabour him.

As Qin Zhong turned to watch the onslaught, he heard a rushing noise behind his head and a square inkstone launched by an unseen hand sailed past it and landed on the desk occupied by Jia Lan and Jia Jun.

Jia Lan and Jia Jun belonged to the Rong-guo half

of the clan and were in the same generation as the other Jia Lan, the little son of Li Wan and nephew of Bao-yu. Jia Jun had lost his father in infancy and was doted on by his widowed mother. Jia Lan was his best friend, which is why they always sat next to each other in school. Though Jia Jun was among the youngest in the class, his tiny body contained an heroic soul. He was extremely mischievous and completely fearless. With the impartial interest of an observer he had watched a friend of Jokey Jin's slyly aim the inkstone at Tealeaf; but when it fell short and landed right in front of him on his own desk, smashing a porcelain water-bottle and showering his books with inky water, his blood was up.

'Rotten swine!' he shouted. 'If this is a free-for-all, here goes!' and he grabbed at the inkstone intending to send it sailing back. But Jia Lan was a man of peace and held it firmly down.

'Leave it, old chap! It's none of our business,' he counselled.

Jia Jun was not to be restrained, however. Deprived of the inkstone, he picked up a satchel full of books and raising it in both hands above his head, hurled it in the direction of the assailant. Unfortunately his body was too small and his strength too puny for so great a trajectory, and the satchel fell on the desk occupied by Bao-yu and Qin Zhong. It landed with a tremendous crash, scattering books, papers, writing-brushes and inkstones in all directions and smashing Bao-yu's tea-bowl to simthereens so that tea flowed over everything round about. Nothing daunted, Jia Jun leaped out and rushed upon the thrower of inkstones to smite him.

Meanwhile Jokey Jin had found a bamboo pole which he flailed around him: a terrible weapon in so confined and crowded a space. Soon Tealeaf had sustained a blow from it and was bawling for reinforcements from outside. There were three other pages in attendance on Bao-yu besides himself, all equally inclined to mischief. Their names were Sweeper, Ploughboy and Inky. With a great shout of 'To arms! To arms! Down with the bastards!' these three now came rushing like angry hornets into the classroom, Inky wielding a door-bar which he had picked up and Sweeper and Ploughboy brandishing horsewhips.

Jia Rui, in a frenzy of outraged authority, hopped from one to the other, alternately grabbing and cajoling, but none would take the slightest bit of notice. Disorder was now general. The more mischievous of the scholars mingled gleefully in the fray, safe, in the general scrimmage, to land punches at chosen foes without fear of discovery or reprisal. The more timid crawled into places of safety. Others stood on their desks, laughing and clapping their hands and cheering on the combatants. The classroom was like a cauldron of still water that had suddenly come to the boil.

Li Gui and the other older servants, hearing the up-roar from outside, now hurried in, and by concerted shouting eventually managed to call the boys to a halt. Li Gui asked them what they were fighting about. He was answered by a medley of voices, some saying one thing and some another. Unable to make sense of what he heard, he turned his attention to Tealeaf and the other pages, cursing them roundly and turning them out of the room.

Qin Zhong had fallen an early victim to Jokey Jin's pole, sustaining a nasty graze on the head which Bao-yu was at this very moment mopping with the flap of his gown. Seeing that Li Gui had succeeded in re-storing some kind of order, he asked to be taken away.

'Pack up my books, Li Gui, and fetch the horse, will you? I am going to tell Great-uncle Dai-ru about this. We were shamefully insulted, and because we didn't

77

want to start a quarrel, we went along in a perfectly polite and reasonable manner and reported the matter to Cousin Rui. But instead of doing anything about it, he gave *us* a telling-off, stood by while someone called us filthy names, and actually *encouraged* them to start hitting us. Naturally Tealeaf stuck up for us when he saw we were being bullied. What would you expect him to do? But they all ganged up on him and started hitting *him*, and even Qin Zhong's head was cut open. We can't go on studying here after this.'

Li Gui tried to calm him.

'Don't be hasty, young master! Your great-uncle has gone home on business and if we go running after him to pester him about a little thing like this, he'll think we don't know how to behave. If you want my advice, the proper way to settle this affair is by dealing with it here, where it started. Not by rushing off and upsetting your poor old uncle.' He turned to Jia Rui. 'This is all your fault, Mr. Rui, sir. While your granfer is away you are the head of the whole school and everyone looks to you to set an example. If anyone does anything they shouldn't, it's up to you to deal with it— give them a hiding, or whatever it is they need. Not sit by and let matters get out of hand to this extent.'

'I *did* tell them to stop,' said Jia Rui, 'but they wouldn't listen.'

'If you don't mind my saying so,' said Li Gui, 'it's because you've been to blame yourself on past occasions that these lads won't do what you tell them to now. So if this business today does get to the ears of your grandfather, you'll be in trouble yourself, along of all the rest. If I were you, sir, I should think of some way of sorting this out as quickly as possible.'

'Sort it out nothing!' said Bao-yu. 'I'm definitely going to report this.'

'If Jokey Jin stays here,' wailed Qin Zhong tearfully, 'I'm not studying in this school any longer.'

'There is no earthly reason to talk about leaving this school,' said Bao-yu. 'We have as much right to come here as anyone else. When I've explained to everyone exactly what happened, Jokey Jin will be expelled.

'Who is this Jokey Jin, any way?' he asked Li Gui.

Li Gui thought for a moment.

'Better not ask. If I told you, it would only make for more unpleasantness.'

Tealeaf's voice piped up from outside the window:

'He's the nephew of Mrs Huang on the Ning-guo side. Trash like that trying to scare us! I know your

Auntie Huang, Jokey Jin! She's an old scrounger. I've seen her down on her knees in front of our Mrs Lian, begging for stuff so that she could go out and pawn it. What an aunt! I'd be ashamed to own an aunt like that!'

Li Gui shouted at him furiously.

'Detestable little varmint! Trust *you* to know the answer and spread your poison!'

Bao-yu sniffed contemptuously.

'So that's who he is! The nephew of Cousin Huang's wife. I'll go and speak to *her* about this.'

He wanted to go straight away, and called to Tealeaf to come inside and pack up his books.

'No need for you to go, Master Bao,' said Tealeaf as he swaggered in triumphantly to do his bidding. 'Let me go for you and save you the trouble. I'll just say that Lady Jia wants a word with her, hire a carriage, and bring her along myself. Then you can question her in front of Lady Jia.'

Li Gui was furious.

'Do you want to die? If you're not careful, my lad, when we get home I'll first thrash the living daylights out of you and then tell Sir Zheng and Lady Wang that Master Bao was put up to all this by your provocation.

I've had trouble enough as it is trying to get these lads calmed down a bit without needing any fresh trouble from you. It was all of your making, this rumpus, in the first place. But instead of thinking about ways of damping it down, you have to go throwing more fat on the fire.'

After this outburst Tealeaf was at last silent.

Jia Rui was by now terrified lest the matter should go any further and his own far from clean record be brought to light. Fear made him abject. Addressing Qin Zhong and Bao-yu in turn, he humbly begged them not to report it. At first they were adamant. Then Bao-yu made a condition:

'All right, we won't tell. But you must make Jokey Jin apologize.'

At first Jokey Jin refused, but Jia Rui was insistent, and Li Gui added his own persuasion:

'After all, it started with you, so if you don't do what they say, how are we ever going to end it?'

Under their combined pressure Jokey Jin's resistance at last gave way and he locked hands and made Qin Zhong a bow. But Bao-yu said this was not enough. He insisted on a kotow. Jia Rui, whose only concern now was to get the matter over with as quickly as possible, quietly urged him to comply:

'You know what the proverb says:

> He who can check a moment's rage
> Shall calm and carefree end his days.'

APOLLONIUS OF RHODES · *Jason and the Argonauts*
ARISTOPHANES · *Lysistrata*
SAINT AUGUSTINE · *Confessions of a Sinner*
JANE AUSTEN · *The History of England*
HONORÉ DE BALZAC · *The Atheist's Mass*
BASHŌ · *Haiku*
AMBROSE BIERCE · *An Occurrence at Owl Creek Bridge*
JAMES BOSWELL · *Meeting Dr Johnson*
CHARLOTTE BRONTË · *Mina Laury*
CAO XUEQIN · *The Dream of the Red Chamber*
THOMAS CARLYLE · *On Great Men*
BALDESAR CASTIGLIONE · *Etiquette for Renaissance Gentlemen*
CERVANTES · *The Jealous Extremaduran*
KATE CHOPIN · *The Kiss and Other Stories*
JOSEPH CONRAD · *The Secret Sharer*
DANTE · *The First Three Circles of Hell*
CHARLES DARWIN · *The Galapagos Islands*
THOMAS DE QUINCEY · *The Pleasures and Pains of Opium*
DANIEL DEFOE · *A Visitation of the Plague*
BERNAL DÍAZ · *The Betrayal of Montezuma*
FYODOR DOSTOYEVSKY · *The Gentle Spirit*
FREDERICK DOUGLASS · *The Education of Frederick Douglass*
GEORGE ELIOT · *The Lifted Veil*
GUSTAVE FLAUBERT · *A Simple Heart*
BENJAMIN FRANKLIN · *The Means and Manner of Obtaining Virtue*
EDWARD GIBBON · *Reflections on the Fall of Rome*
CHARLOTTE PERKINS GILMAN · *The Yellow Wallpaper*
GOETHE · *Letters from Italy*
HOMER · *The Rage of Achilles*
HOMER · *The Voyages of Odysseus*

PENGUIN 60s CLASSICS

HENRY JAMES · *The Lesson of the Master*
FRANZ KAFKA · *The Judgement* and *In the Penal Colony*
THOMAS À KEMPIS · *Counsels on the Spiritual Life*
HEINRICH VON KLEIST · *The Marquise of O—*
LIVY · *Hannibal's Crossing of the Alps*
NICCOLÒ MACHIAVELLI · *The Art of War*
SIR THOMAS MALORY · *The Death of King Arthur*
GUY DE MAUPASSANT · *Boule de Suif*
FRIEDRICH NIETZSCHE · *Zarathustra's Discourses*
OVID · *Orpheus in the Underworld*
PLATO · *Phaedrus*
EDGAR ALLAN POE · *The Murders in the Rue Morgue*
ARTHUR RIMBAUD · *A Season in Hell*
JEAN-JACQUES ROUSSEAU · *Meditations of a Solitary Walker*
ROBERT LOUIS STEVENSON · *Dr Jekyll and Mr Hyde*
TACITUS · *Nero and the Burning of Rome*
HENRY DAVID THOREAU · *Civil Disobedience* and *Reading*
LEO TOLSTOY · *The Death of Ivan Ilyich*
IVAN TURGENEV · *Three Sketches from a Hunter's Album*
MARK TWAIN · *The Man That Corrupted Hadleyburg*
GIORGIO VASARI · *Lives of Three Renaissance Artists*
EDITH WHARTON · *Souls Belated*
WALT WHITMAN · *Song of Myself*
OSCAR WILDE · *The Portrait of Mr W. H.*

ANONYMOUS WORKS

Beowulf and Grendel
Buddha's Teachings
Gilgamesh and Enkidu

Krishna's Dialogue on the Soul
Tales of Cú Chulaind
Two Viking Romances

READ MORE IN PENGUIN

For complete information about books available from Penguin and how to order them, please write to us at the appropriate address below. Please note that for copyright reasons the selection of books varies from country to country.

IN THE UNITED KINGDOM: Please write to *Dept. JC, Penguin Books Ltd, FREEPOST, West Drayton, Middlesex UB7 OBR.*
If you have any difficulty in obtaining a title, please send your order with the correct money, plus ten per cent for postage and packaging, to *PO Box No. 11, West Drayton, Middlesex UB7 OBR.*

IN THE UNITED STATES: Please write to *Consumer Sales, Penguin USA, P.O. Box 999, Dept. 17109, Bergenfield, New Jersey 07621-0120.* VISA and MasterCard holders call 1-800-253-6476 to order all Penguin titles.

IN CANADA: Please write to *Penguin Books Canada Ltd, 10 Alcorn Avenue, Suite 300, Toronto, Ontario M4V 3B2.*

IN AUSTRALIA: Please write to *Penguin Books Australia Ltd, P.O. Box 257, Ringwood, Victoria 3134.*

IN NEW ZEALAND: Please write to *Penguin Books (NZ) Ltd, Private Bag 102902, North Shore Mail Centre, Auckland 10.*

IN INDIA: Please write to *Penguin Books India Pvt Ltd, 706 Eros Apartments, 56 Nehru Place, New Delhi 110 019.*

IN THE NETHERLANDS: Please write to *Penguin Books Netherlands bv, Postbus 3507, NL-1001 AH Amsterdam.*

IN GERMANY: Please write to *Penguin Books Deutschland GmbH, Metzlerstrasse 26, 60594 Frankfurt am Main.*

IN SPAIN: Please write to *Penguin Books S. A., Bravo Murillo 19, 1o B, 28015 Madrid.*

IN ITALY: Please write to *Penguin Italia s.r.l., Via Felice Casati 20, I-20124 Milano.*

IN FRANCE: Please write to *Penguin France S. A., 17 rue Lejeune, F-31000 Toulouse.*

IN JAPAN: Please write to *Penguin Books Japan, Ishikiribashi Building, 2-5-4, Suido, Bunkyo-ku, Tokyo 112.*

IN GREECE: Please write to *Penguin Hellas Ltd, Dimocritou 3, GR-106 71 Athens.*

IN SOUTH AFRICA: Please write to *Longman Penguin Southern Africa (Pty) Ltd, Private Bag X08, Bertsham 2013.*